SUPERHERO SCIENCE

SHAPESHIFTING

BLASTOFF! DISCOVERY

BY BLAKE HOENA

BELLWETHER MEDIA • MINNEAPOLIS, MN

Blastoff! Discovery launches a new mission: reading to learn. Filled with facts and features, each book offers you an exciting new world to explore!

This edition first published in 2022 by Bellwether Media, Inc.

Library of Congress Cataloging-in-Publication Data

LC record for Shapeshifting available at:
https://lccn.loc.gov/2021049550

Editor: Elizabeth Neuenfeldt   Designer: Andrea Schneider

Printed in the United States of America, North Mankato, MN.

TABLE OF CONTENTS

A PAIR OF SHAPESHIFTERS

It is a sunny afternoon in San Francisco, California. Hope van Dyne and Scott Lang are enjoying lunch together. From the restaurant, they have a view of San Francisco Bay stretching out before them.

While eating, they notice something strange. A ship full of passengers is starting to tip over. The ship is going to sink! The pair leaps into action. Secretly, they are the superheroes the Wasp and Ant-Man. They have special suits that give them the **ability** to shapeshift.

FIRST APPEARANCES

- **Ant-Man first appeared in the comic *Tales to Astonish* issue number 27 in 1962. The Wasp joined Ant-Man about one year later!**

The Wasp and Ant-Man both shrink down to the size of bugs. The Wasp flies out toward the sinking ship. Ant-Man calls to a winged ant. He rides on its back.

Once the heroes reach the ship, the Wasp lands on its deck. She keeps passengers from falling overboard. Ant-Man dives into the water. Then, he increases his size to 10 times larger than normal. He stands in the water and pushes the ship upright so it does not sink. With their superpowers, the Wasp and Ant-Man save the day!

SUPERHERO FAMILY

- Hope van Dyne is the daughter of Janet van Dyne and Henry Pym. Janet was the original Wasp while Henry was the original Ant-Man.

THE POWER OF SHAPESHIFTING

Shapeshifting is a common superpower. Heroes like Ant-Man and the Wasp can change their size. Others can shapeshift into other people or animals. Some superheroes, such as Elastigirl and Plastic Man, can stretch their bodies to amazing lengths!

In the 1940s, DC Comics created Plastic Man. He was once a thief named Patrick O'Brian. But then he fell into strange chemicals. This gave him the ability to change the shape of his body. Patrick decided to use this new power to fight crime as Plastic Man.

PLASTIC MAN

SUPERHERO PROFILE

SUPERHERO NAME Beast Boy

REAL NAME Garfield Logan

SUPERPOWERS

shapeshifting, super strength, super speed

BACKSTORY

When he was young, Garfield became ill with a rare disease. He was given experimental medicine as a cure. It turned his skin and hair green. It also gave him the ability to change into animal shapes.

SELECT APPEARANCES

- *Doom Patrol* comics issue number 99 **(1965)**
- *The New Teen Titans* comics **(1980 TO 1984)**
- *Teen Titans Go!* cartoon **(2013 TO PRESENT)**
- *Teen Titans GO! to the Movies* feature film **(2018)**

Martian Manhunter is a mighty superhero from Mars. He was made by DC Comics in the 1950s. He was born with superpowers. He is super strong and tough to hurt. When not fighting crime, Martian Manhunter uses his shapeshifting ability to appear human.

In the 1960s, Mr. Fantastic was introduced to Marvel comic book readers. After being struck by **radiation**, he gained the ability to stretch his body almost any way he wants. Around this time, DC created Beast Boy. He can change into different animals!

ANTIHERO

- Mystique is a well-known shapeshifting enemy of the X-Men. But she has used her abilities to help them. She even saved Professor X, the leader of the X-Men!

MYSTIQUE

MR. FANTASTIC

MEDIA MANIA!

TV SERIES *Adventure Time*

YEARS 2010 to 2018

DESCRIPTION

Finn the Human and Jake the Dog go on crazy adventures in the futuristic Land of Ooo. Jake has the ability to shapeshift. He can change his size and his shape. Jake has turned himself into a sailboat and a parachute!

In the 1990s, Copycat appeared in Marvel comic books. She is a **mutant** who shapeshifts to look like other people. She can also copy their abilities. Once, she copied another hero's healing ability to heal herself after an injury.

Teenager Kamala Khan is one of the newest superheroes. She became Ms. Marvel in 2014. She can stretch out her body and make her fists huge to fight evil villains. Kamala is the first **Muslim** superhero to have her own Marvel comic book series!

CHANGING ROLES

▸ Carol Danvers was once Ms. Marvel. But when she became Captain Marvel, Kamala Khan took on the role of Ms. Marvel.

KAMALA KHAN AS MS. MARVEL

CAROL DANVERS AS CAPTAIN MARVEL

EVERYDAY SHAPESHIFTING

People have found many ways to change their appearances. Hundreds of years ago, **Scandinavian** warriors wore wolf skins to look like wolves. They would even act like wolves! The warriors believed their appearance would frighten enemies.

Today's soldiers wear **camouflage** to hide their appearance. Their clothing often has similar colors and patterns to their surroundings. **Ghillie suits** are an advanced form of camouflage. These outfits are made to copy the shape and movements of things found in nature. A person wearing a ghillie suit might look like clumps of grass or a leafy bush.

WEREBEASTS

WERETIGER

- There are many stories about shapeshifting creatures. In Europe and North America, people tell tales of werewolves. In Asia, there are legends of weretigers. In Africa, people talk of wereleopards!

GHILLIE SUIT

For thousands of years, people have used makeup to change their appearances. Modern makeup can completely **alter** what a person looks like. It can even make a person's facial features appear to be different shapes.

Prosthetics take makeup to the next level. These fake body parts might be a rubber nose or a body suit with muscles. In movies, actors wear prosthetic makeup to look like otherworldly creatures. They can have pointed ears to look like elves. They can have horrible injuries to appear like zombies. Prosthetics can make people look like almost anything!

COSPLAY

- Many fans of games, movies, and books are cosplayers. Cosplayers wear makeup and costumes to look like their favorite characters!

SHAPESHIFTING IN NATURE

SOME ANIMALS HAVE SHAPESHIFTING ABILITIES!

PUFFERFISH

WHEN THREATENED, THEY PUFF UP TO MORE THAN DOUBLE THEIR SIZE

MIMIC OCTOPUSES

THEY CAN LOOK AND ACT LIKE OTHER ANIMALS, SUCH AS SEA SNAKES OR LIONFISH

MUTABLE RAINFROGS

THEY CAN CHANGE THE TEXTURE OF THEIR SKIN

Today, technology can completely change the appearance of an actor. **Motion capture** uses **sensors** placed on an actor's body. These sensors **digitally** record the actor's movements. With **CGI** software, **animators** use these recordings to alter an actor's appearance.

Motion capture and CGI are often used in movies and video games. This technology can make an actor look like an otherworldly hero or an evil monster. It can make an actor look younger, older, or like a realistic animated character.

THE SCIENCE BEHIND MOTION CAPTURE AND CGI

1 An actor films a scene while wearing motion capture sensors

2 A camera tracks the movements of the actor with the help of the sensors

3 The sensors create a digital model of the actor and their movements

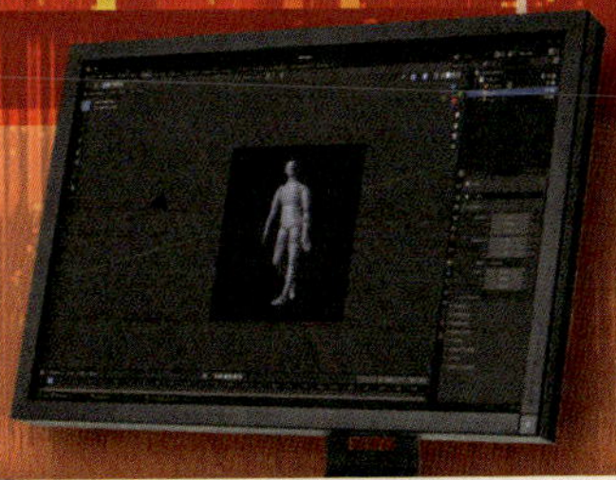

4 Animators use CGI software to change the appearance of the digital model of the actor

5 The actor now looks completely different on screen

SHORTEN IT UP

- **Many technology terms have shortened names. CGI is short for computer-generated imagery. Motion capture is often shortened to mo-cap!**

IS SHAPESHIFTING POSSIBLE?

CONTORTIONIST

Some people can move their bodies in amazing ways. **Contortionists** are very **flexible**. They can wrap their legs over their heads. Some can fold their bodies to fit into tiny spaces. But their abilities cannot match that of a superhero like Mr. Fantastic.

A person would be in extreme pain having their arms or legs pulled just a few inches. If a person tried to twist their body like Plastic Man, they would hurt themselves. They would tear skin and break bones.

ILLUSTRATION OF A NUCLEAR BOMB

Changing size like Ant-Man would be just as impossible. To become larger or smaller, a person would have to alter their **mass**. Mass is the amount of matter that makes up an object.

It takes a lot of **energy** to change the mass of something. For a person to shrink down to the size of a cat, they would need to create energy equal to a **nuclear bomb**. The release of that energy would destroy everything around them! If the person survived the change, they would not be able to change back.

NEGATIVE EFFECTS OF SHAPESHIFTING

STRETCHING OUT BODY

EFFECTS:
- TORN SKIN
- BROKEN BONES

BECOMING SMALL

EFFECTS:
- COULD NOT BECOME LARGE AGAIN
- ENERGY NEEDED WOULD DESTROY SURROUNDINGS

It is difficult to change the shapes of living things. But scientists have discovered a way to shapeshift non-living materials. In 2018, scientists at University of Colorado Boulder made a material that changes shape using temperature and light. Scientists can **program** the material to change its shape!

When heat is added, the material can change into a certain shape. When heat is removed, the material will change back to its original shape. Scientists hope these materials can be used in medical devices and **3D printing**.

THE FUTURE OF SHAPESHIFTING

People will likely never have the ability to shapeshift like a superhero. But scientists are looking into new and exciting ways to create shapeshifting technology.

In the future, people may use shapeshifting robots. NASA has begun developing robots that can shapeshift. They will be able to change from a flying **drone** to a rolling ball. They could even swim underwater. One day, these robots might be used to explore and learn about Saturn's moons!

ILLUSTRATION OF THE SURFACE OF SATURN'S MOON, TITAN

SPACE EXPLORERS

- NASA stands for National Aeronautics and Space Administration. It is the United States government agency in charge of space exploration!

ILLUSTRATION OF A SHAPESHIFTING ROBOT

AUDI SKYSPHERE

One day, people may drive around with shapeshifting cars. In 2021, Audi introduced a new car idea called the skysphere. This car might change from a self-driven car to a human-driven car. It also could change its size by 10 inches (25 centimeters)!

People have long had ways of changing their appearances. With new advancements in makeup and prosthetics, those alterations are becoming even more amazing. In the future, people may use shapeshifting technologies to explore the world around them!

PROSTHETIC MASKS

GLOSSARY

3D printing—the production of solid objects by using layers of a material based on a specific pattern or model

ability—the power to do something

alter—to change

animators—artists who create cartoons

camouflage—colors or patterns that blend in with surroundings

CGI—computer-generated imagery; CGI is artwork created by computers.

contortionists—performers who twist their bodies into unusual positions

digitally—relating to something that uses computer technology

drone—an aircraft that is flown by a remote control or by computers

energy—the power needed to do something

flexible—bendable

ghillie suits—suits that are worn to camouflage someone by making them look like something in nature, such as grass or shrubs

mass—the amount of matter that makes up something

motion capture—a technology that matches human movement to computer-generated characters

Muslim—related to a person who practices the Islamic faith

mutant—a human who was born with superpowers in Marvel Comics

nuclear bomb—a bomb that produces a very powerful explosion

program—to give something a certain set of instructions in order for it to perform a specific task

prosthetics—fake body parts made from rubber or other materials

radiation—powerful energy that comes from a source in the form of waves or particles that cannot be seen

Scandinavian—related to people from the countries of Denmark, Norway, and Sweden

sensors—devices that detect or sense heat, light, sound, or motion and react to it in a certain way

TO LEARN MORE

AT THE LIBRARY

Hoena, Blake. *Invisibility*. Minneapolis, Minn.: Bellwether Media, 2021.

Loh-Hagan, Virginia. *Weird Science. Movies*. Ann Arbor, Mich.: Cherry Lake Publishing, 2022.

Parks, Spencer. *Robots in Space*. New York, N.Y.: Cavendish Square Publishing, 2022.

ON THE WEB

FACTSURFER

Factsurfer.com gives you a safe, fun way to find more information.

1. Go to www.factsurfer.com.
2. Enter "shapeshifting" into the search box and click 🔍.
3. Select your book cover to see a list of related content.

INDEX

The images in this book are reproduced through the courtesy of: Album/ Alamy, front cover, pp. 13 (Carol Danvers), 31; EdmondP, p. 3; Collection Christophel/ Alamy, pp. 4-5 (Ant-Man and the Wasp); Marvel/ Walt Disney Studios Motion Pictures/ Everett Collection, p. 5; Moviestore Collection Ltd/ Alamy, pp. 6-7, 7, 19 (CGI); Allstar Picture Library Limited/ Alamy, pp. 8-9 (Elastigirl), 19 (step 5); Danny1999, p. 9 (Plastic Man); AA Film Archive/ Alamy, p. 10 (Beast Boy); TCD/Prod.DB/ Alamy, p. 11 (Mystique); Photo 12/ Alamy, pp. 10-11 (Mr. Fantastic); Cartoon Network/ PhotofestNYC, p. 12 (*Adventure Time*); Getmilitaryphotos, p. 14 (desert camouflage, snow camouflage); DomCritelli, p. 15 (weretiger); Volodymyr Burdiak, pp. 14-15 (ghillie suit); Sun Shock, p. 16 (prosthetic makeup); PJ_Photography, p. 17 (cosplay); IrinaK, p. 17 (pufferfish); Ethan Daniels, p. 17 (mimic octopuses); Morley Read/ Alamy, p. 17 (mutable rainfrogs); Gorodenkoff, p. 18; andreyuu, p. 19 (girl, step 1, 2); Gino Stanta Maria, p. 19 (camera, step 2, 3); rangizzz, p. 19 (step 4); Nguyen van vien, pp. 20-21 (contortionist); inkspotzs, p. 21 (Mr. Fantastic); James Thew/ Alamy, pp. 22-23 (nuclear bomb); MiguelMalo, p. 24 (University of Colorado Boulder); Artshake Media, pp. 24-25 (3D printer); Dotted Yeti, p. 26 (Titan); Thomas Marek, p. 27 (NASA); NASA_JPL-Caltech/ NASA, p. 27 (shapeshifting robots); Jurik Peter p. 26-27; Audi Newsroom/ Audi Newsroom, pp. 28-29 (Audi skysphere); Tara Ziemba/ Getty Images, p. 29 (prosthetic masks).